Does it sound like the ocean
and remind you of the waves?

Does it feel like the wind
before a big storm

or the breeze at the start of spring?

As you take your next breath,
begin to notice the sounds around you.

Can you hear the cars passing by outside your window?
Can you hear the *whirr* of a laundry machine
or the *hum* of a motor?

HUMMED

WHIRR

And what about
the thoughts in your head?

Do they make sounds?
Do they have names?

Are some of your thoughts big?
Are some of them small?

See if you can imagine what they look like.
See if you can picture them moving across your mind.

Now take a big breath
and pretend you can
let go of each of those thoughts.

Imagine your breath is the wind
and your thoughts are the clouds.

whoosh.

Follow your breath down into your arms.
Feel the breath flow into your hands,

maybe all
the way down
to the tips of
your fingers.

Wow, that is
a long way
from your nose!

Take another big, slow breath of air.
This time let it fill your lungs
like two big balloons at a party.

**And imagine your heart is a beautiful present
sitting between those two balloons.**

Imagine yourself unwrapping that present.

Imagine the smiles around you,

the laughter,

your excitement.

What do you find inside?

A word,

a memory, a friendship?

Let that feeling of surprise fill your whole body.

Now, when you are ready, but only when you are ready,
take another big breath. (You're getting good at this!)

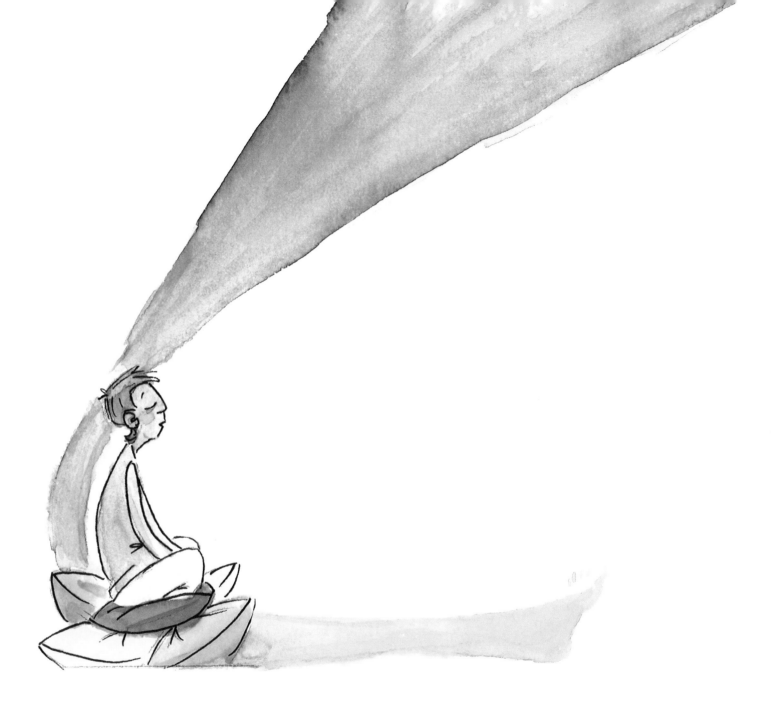

And this time, follow it down your spine, through
your legs, and down to the tips of your toes.

Can you remember all the places you have been today?
Imagine all the invisible footprints you have left behind.

Then take another big breath,
and let them all go,
like footprints washed
away by the waves.

Let go of the day. Let go of the
coulds, the *woulds*, and the *shoulds*,
the goods and the bads.

And for a moment,

just

BREATHE

Breathe in the blue sky of your mind.

Breathe in the light of your heart.

Breathe in the tingling of your toes

and the warmth in your hands.

Breathe in all you are

and all you will be.

Breathe in everywhere you've been

and everywhere you'll go.

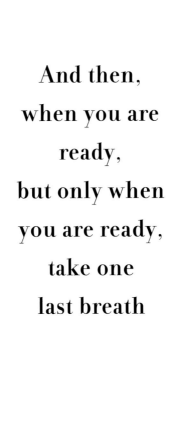

And then,
when you are
ready,
but only when
you are ready,
take one
last breath

and open your eyes.

How do you feel on the inside?

How do you feel on the outside?

Do you feel lighter, more relaxed,
maybe a little calmer?

May you carry this feeling with you

through your day and your dreams.

And may you share it with everyone you meet!

• Author's Note •

Hi. My name is Bill. I'm a teacher, a student, a writer, and most of all, a meditator. I wrote this book to help meditators both young and old, but especially young. Over the years, meditation has brought me so much joy, and I hope to share some of it with you in these pages. Meditation has helped me stay calm when things got overwhelming, it has helped me let go of thoughts that sometimes got stuck in my head, and most of all, it has helped me open up my heart when I needed to be brave. Meditation brings countless other benefits, like better sleep, better focus, and better behavior in school. I'm not sure what you will find at the other end of this journey, but I hope this book will be the start of a lifelong practice, and maybe, just maybe, it will offer you one or two benefits that no one else has discovered.

Enjoy!

Photo © Emily Wilson

WILLIAM MEYER is a high school teacher, longtime meditator, and the author of *Three Breaths and Begin: A Guide to Meditation in the Classroom*, among other books.

billpmeyer.com

BRITTANY R. JACOBS is the author of *The Kraken's Rules for Making Friends* and is a children's book author/illustrator and librarian.

brittanyrjacobs.com

New World Library
www.newworldlibrary.com

Text copyright © 2019 by William Meyer

Illustrations copyright © 2019 by Brittany R. Jacobs

Library of Congress Cataloging-in-Publication data is available.

First printing, August 2019

ISBN 978-1-60868-633-9
Ebook ISBN 978-1-60868-634-6

Printed in Canada

10   9   8   7   6   5   4   3   2   1